MY FIVE SENSES

BY MARGARET MILLER

Aladdin Paperbacks

For my mother,
who always encouraged me to see

ACKNOWLEDGMENTS
My special thanks to the children in this book:
Miranda Berman, Annie Bernard, Rafael Espaillat,
Max and Gus Halper, Gideon Jacobs, and Morgan Means. –M. M.

First Aladdin Paperbacks edition July 1998
Copyright © 1994 by Margaret Miller

Aladdin Paperbacks
An imprint of Simon & Schuster Children's Publishing Division
1230 Avenue of the Americas
New York, NY 10020

Also available in a Simon & Schuster
Books for Young Readers hardcover edition.
Designed by Sylvia Frezzolini
Manufactured in China
30 29 28 27 26

The Library of Congress has cataloged the
hardcover edition as follows:
Miller, Margaret.
My five senses / by Margaret Miller. p. cm.
Summary: A simple introduction to the five senses
and how they help us experience the world around us.
ISBN 978-0-671-79168-1
1. Senses and sensation—Juvenile literature. [1. Senses and sensation.]
I. Title.
QP434.M55   1993   93-1956
612.8—dc20   CIP
ISBN 978-0-689-82009-0 (pbk.)
1213 SCP

I have two eyes, a nose,

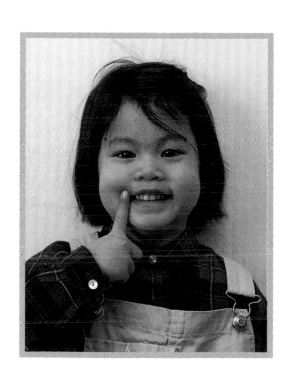  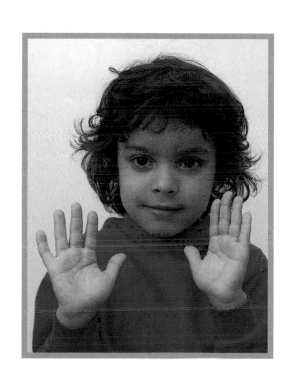

a mouth, two ears, and two hands.

With my eyes I see myself,

my shadow,

my dog,

and my city.

With my nose I smell popcorn,

a horse,

flowers,

and garbage.

With my mouth I taste watermelon,

the ocean,

medicine,

and ice cream.

With my ears I hear my baby brother,

a fire engine,

my piano,

and whispered secrets.

With my hands I feel finger paints,

sand,

water,

and a rabbit.

With our five senses, we enjoy our world.